For Mr and Mrs B
and for Zeke ... their dog.

Our Bloomsbury Book House
has a special room for each
age group -
this one is from the Nursery.

First Published in Great Britain in 1995
Bloomsbury Publishing Plc, 38 Soho Square, London W1V 5DF
This edition published 1997

Copyright © Text and illustrations Bernice Lum 1995
The moral right of the author has been asserted
A CIP catalogue record of this book is available from the
British Library

ISBN 0 7475 3067 X

Manufactured in China

10 9 8 7 6 5 4 3 2 1

Gamesroom
ages 9 +

Bedroom
ages 6 – 9

Playroom
ages 4 – 7

Nursery
ages 1 – 4

If My Dog Went on Holiday

Bernice Lum

Bloomsbury Children's Books

If my dog went on holiday ...

he would go to the seaside.

He would build sandcastles ...

go for a swim ...

or a float ...

and maybe bury a friend.

He could go snorkelling ...

collect shells and rocks ...

and could even go rowing.

He might go waterskiing ...

and windsurfing ...

or just lie in the sun.

Best of all he would like to sit on my towel ...

and eat my ice cream.